Hector's
Favorite Place

For all the little worriers out there...myself included!—JR

Published by
MAGINATION PRESS®
American Psychological Association
750 First Street NE
Washington, DC 20002

Magination Press is a registered trademark of the
American Psychological Association.
For more information about our books, including a complete catalog,
please write to us, call 1-800-374-2721, or visit our website at
www.apa.org/pubs/magination.

Book design by Susan K. White
Printed by Worzalla, Stevens Point, WI

Library of Congress Cataloging-in-Publication Data
Names: Rooks, Jo, author.
Title: Hector's Favorite Place / by Jo Rooks.
Description: Washington, DC : Magination Press, [2018]
Identifiers: LCCN 2017044133| ISBN 9781433828683 (hardcover)
  ISBN 1433828685 (hardcover)
Subjects: LCSH: Bashfulness—Juvenile literature. | Self-confidence—
  Juvenile literature. | Friendship—Juvenile literature.
Classification: LCC BF575.B3 R57 2018 | DDC 155.4/192—dc23 LC
record available at https://lccn.loc.gov/2017044133

Manufactured in the United States of America
10 9 8 7 6 5 4 3 2 1

Hector's
Favorite Place

Jo Rooks

MAGINATION PRESS · WASHINGTON, DC

American Psychological Association

Hector loved his home. It was his **favorite place** to be.

At home,

there was always...

so **much** to do.

Hector loved his home so much that he didn't often go out. Home was cozy and snuggly and safe.

But Hector liked to hear all the news of the forest when his friends came to visit.

One day, Hector was just having a little nap when there was a knock at the door.

"Hector, have you seen?
It's snowing outside!"
said Archie. "Let's go for
a walk in the forest
and make footprints!"

"Jumping June bugs!"
said Hector. "So it is!" And
he ran off to find his boots.

But then Hector began to worry.
What if he got cold and caught the flu?

"Er...sorry, Archie, I can't," said Hector.
"I've got so much to do. Maybe tomorrow."

"What a shame," said Archie.

The next day, Hector was reading his new book
when the phone rang.

"Hello, Hector! Have you heard? The lake has frozen!" said Max. "Would you like to come ice skating?"

"Hopping honeybees!" said Hector.

Hector used to go skating when he was small. It was so much fun.

Hector was just
about to say yes when
he began to worry.

What if he had
forgotten how to skate?

He could fall over
and hurt himself.

"Erm...sorry, Max, I can't.
I've got **so much** to do.
Maybe tomorrow."

"What a shame!" said Max.

Later on, Hector was just tucking into his favorite supper when a letter landed on the door mat.

Dear Hector,
You are invited to the

Winter Forest
Party

There will be Music, Dancing,
and Hot Chocolate for everyone!

Tomorrow at 10 o'clock

"That sounds like fun!" thought Hector.

But then Hector began to worry.

He worried about going into
the forest far from home.
"What if I get lost?"
he thought.

He worried about the music.
"What if it's too loud?"
he thought.

He worried about the dancing.
"What if I can't dance?"
he thought.

He even worried
about the hot chocolate.
"What if it's too hot?"
he thought.

CAUTION: HOT!

"I will have to say I'm too busy
to go," sighed Hector,
and he decided to go to bed.

That night, Hector didn't sleep very well. Archie and Max were sure to be at the party. Would they be sad if Hector wasn't there?

Hector knew deep down that his worries were stopping him from going and enjoying himself. He realized he had to be brave.

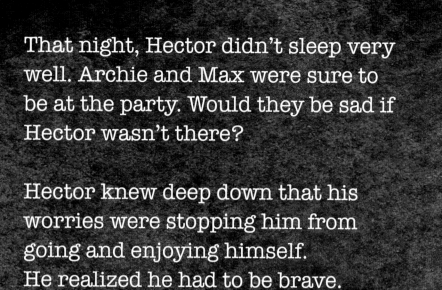

Dear Hector,

You are invited to the

Winter Forest Party

There will be Music, Dancing
and Hot Chocolate for everyone!

Tomorrow at 10 o'clock

In the morning, Hector put on his best bow tie.

"You can do this!" he said to himself.

"What a lovely day for a party!" thought Hector
as he strolled proudly along the path.
His boots made big prints in the snow as he went.

He could hear the music playing as he walked
further into the forest. It sounded so beautiful!

crunch

crunch

crunch

to the Forest

Hector came to a clearing
where everyone was dancing
and enjoying themselves.

Hector watched from behind a tree.

"Maybe I should just go home," he thought nervously.

Then, Hector closed his eyes and pictured himself twirling around to the music. Imaginary Hector was the life and soul of the party!

"If only," he thought longingly.

All of a sudden, Hector realized that his feet were tapping along to the beat, his prickles were swaying to the rhythm, and before he knew it...

...he was **dancing!**

Hector enjoyed himself **so much** that his worries didn't seem to matter anymore.

Archie and Max were so pleased
Hector had joined the party.

They drank the last of the
(not too hot) hot chocolate, and the
music came to an end.

Ice skating

...Hector discovered that skating was just as **fun** as he remembered!

And being
a hedgehog...

...meant falling over
didn't hurt one bit!

"Time to go home, Hector," said Archie.

"Your **favorite** place to be," said Max.

Hector thought for a moment.

"I think I've found **another** favorite place to be," he said.

"Now, where shall we go tomorrow?"

Note to Parents, Caregivers, and Professionals

by Julia Martin Burch, PhD

Life is full of uncertainties. Just walking out the front door opens a child to endless possibilities for where the day might take them! Some children adapt easily to this reality, but many children are inherently more cautious and nervous in the face of new experiences. Being cautious is not a bad thing in itself—often it keeps us safe! It's also fine to have "comfort zones" and to enjoy one's favorite places. However, just as Hector worries about getting cold, loud music, and even his hot chocolate being too hot, some children worry about things that are not truly dangerous. This is the fight or flight alarm system in their brain setting off "false alarms." Over time, as a child continues to listen to this false alarm and avoid uncertainty, it becomes harder and harder to try something new, and their world becomes smaller—just as Hector used to love ice skating when he was little, but is now too nervous to go.

Address the Worry (If You Can)

Like Hector and the forest party, a child might worry about a situation for any number of reasons. For example, do they worry that they will fall while ice skating? Not know anyone? Miss their parents too much? Once you have an understanding of what your child is worried about, you can address any misconceptions they might have about a new situation and help them plan for how to approach it gradually.

Checking in about your child's specific worries gives you the opportunity to make sure they understand the facts of a situation and helps prevent their worried imagination from blowing the danger out of proportion. For example, some children worry about a natural disaster befalling their family, particularly after learning about a natural disaster on the news. In this case, you can explain to your child the likelihood of this happening to your family or, if your child is old enough, help them research these topics themselves. You can also explain what your family, as well as your broader community, would do in the case of a natural disaster. Having the facts can often reduce a child's fears about the unknown.

Model and Practice

You are your child's role model for how to approach new or unpredictable situations. If you appear anxious and avoid new situations, your child learns that there is something to fear in the unknown. They also learn that the way to cope with that fear is to avoid uncertainty and stay in their established comfort zones, like Hector does. To model bravery for your child, willingly approach new experiences and stay calm in the face of uncertainty. Your child learns to be calm and open to trying new things by watching you do this. Similarly, you might also consider sharing times when you felt nervous about a new situation, such as your first time going to a sleepover, as well as how you coped with that worry and how it all turned out. This approach teaches your child that it is perfectly normal to feel some tummy butterflies or to wonder what a new experience will be like, *and* that things will most likely turn out okay.

Try Something New

It is wonderful for a child to feel comfortable and cozy in their home—it might even be their favorite place, just like it was for Hector! However, it is equally important for them to be able to try new things and meet new people as part of healthy development. They might even find new favorite places and things to do! To accomplish this, help your child set small goals around new experiences. It can be very overwhelming to imagine staying through an entire party, but your child can slowly work up to that. For example, they could attend the party for the first half hour (with the option of staying longer if they're having fun!). As your child gets more experience approaching unpredictable situations and begins to build their bravery muscles, their time goal can get longer.

Teach children to encourage themselves when they are feeling anxious. You can teach them positive self-talk such as "I can do it," "I've done it before and I can do it again," and "I'll never know if I don't try!" You can also coach an older child to "check the facts" on their worries, such as asking themselves "What's the worst that could happen? Could I handle that?"

Often the worry a child feels in anticipation of a new situation is far worse than the reality. Predict this for them and help them think through how they will handle that rush of anticipatory nerves, like when Hector pauses behind the tree after arriving at the party. As a caretaker, it is important for you to resist the urge to swoop in and save your child in these tough moments, as research suggests that children actually become more anxious over time when their parents overprotect them from difficult emotions or experiences. Instead, support your struggling child from afar with a thumbs up or simple encouragement like "You can do this!" When a parent steps back, the child has an unparalleled opportunity to grow and learn that they can handle new situations and worries on their own.

Resist Reassurance Seeking

It is normal for children to learn about something bad happening and to ask a parent "Will that happen to me?" However, when a child repeatedly seeks reassurance from a parent despite already receiving an answer (such as, "What if I get sick?" "Will you come home after you run errands?" "What if no one plays with me at recess?" "Are you sure you locked the door? What if someone breaks in?"), this can lead to a vicious cycle. When a child seeks and receives reassurance from a parent, they feel better in the short run, but in the long term they do not learn to cope with worry thoughts on their own. They also learn that the only way to feel better when they are anxious is to ask a parent for reassurance. As a result, children's worries actually tend to intensify when they receive repeated reassurance, which ironically increases the frequency of their reassurance-seeking questions.

It is very challenging to set limits with a worried, reassurance-seeking child. To most parents, comforting or reassuring their anxious child is the most natural thing in the world. However, as discussed above, this can actually worsen your child's anxiety in the long run. To reduce your child's reassurance seeking, explain to them that when you answer their worry questions, you are paying attention to the "worry bully" and that you want to pay attention to your brave child. Explain how when you answer their reassurance-seeking questions, it actually makes them worry more in the long run; you might help them notice how the frequency of their questions has increased over time. Make a plan with your child and other family members to slowly reduce the reassurance you provide. For example, when they ask a repetitive worry question, you might say, "I think you know the answer to that," "That sounds like the worry bully talking," or "What do you think will happen? Can you handle it?" It is difficult, but over time your child will rely less and less on reassurance to cope with their anxious thoughts and instead will gradually learn that they can handle them on their own. This will help them feel more competent, independent, and willing to try new things.

Praise Effort and Bravery

Praise your child any time they attempt to do something that makes them uncomfortable, including tolerating not receiving reassurance! Praise tends to reinforce a child most powerfully when it is specific. You might say to your child, "I love how you went to John's birthday party even though you didn't know everyone who would be there!" Additionally, focus on the effort, not the outcome. Even if your child ultimately backs away and does not fully participate in the new situation, praise their willingness to try, as well as any small steps they took towards the new experience, such as "I really liked how willing you were to get in the car and sit in the parking lot outside soccer practice. I know that was hard for you." You can then support your child in thinking through what they might like to do differently the next time. For example, "Maybe next time, you and I can walk to the field together to check it out."

Finally, just as Hector knows deep down that his worries are stopping him from having fun, children often understand that their worries and avoidance behavior are limiting them. Accordingly, when children do face their fears and try something new, they are typically very proud of themselves and want to do it more often. This bravery can have a cumulative effect—the more a child tries new things, the more they learn there is little to fear in the unknown.

Seek Support

If your child's worrying is so intense that it begins to impact their functioning or causes them significant distress, you should consult with a licensed psychologist or other mental health professional who specializes in cognitive behavioral therapy (CBT) for children.

Julia Martin Burch, PhD, is a staff psychologist at the McLean Anxiety Mastery Program at McLean Hospital in Boston. Dr. Martin Burch completed her training at Fairleigh Dickinson University and Massachusetts General Hospital/Harvard Medical School. She works with children, teens, and parents, and specializes in cognitive behavioral therapy for anxiety, obsessive compulsive, and related disorders.

About the Author and Illustrator

JO ROOKS is an illustrator, author, and graphic designer living in South West London with her husband and two children. Jo studied at Bath School of Art and Design and pursued a career in graphic design. When Jo had her two children, she began to rediscover her love of art, poetry, and creative writing for children. She is passionate about reading with children and hopes to bring lovable characters and meaningful messages in her story books.

About Magination Press

MAGINATION PRESS is an imprint of the American Psychological Association, the largest scientific and professional organization representing psychologists in the United States and the largest association of psychologists worldwide.